A CHRISTMAS DELIVERY

AMBER GHE

HUSTLE & WRITE PUBLISHING

Cover Art: Amber Ghe

Editing: Reflected Gifts

ISBN: 978-1-958623-08-4

ISBN: 978-1-958623-09-1

Dedicated to my hubby Larry

A CHRISTMAS DELIVERY

CHAPTER 1

BLAKE

"OH MAN, DO YOU HAVE TO WAKE ME UP SO early?" I said out loud, opening my eyes to my dog Kobe whimpering.

Attempting to wake myself from a deep slumber, I swiped my face. Kobe was running around my room. Running from the bedroom door, then back to me was an indication he wanted to relieve himself.

I blew out air. "Okay, buddy, just give me a second to get myself together."

Swinging my legs over the side of the bed and slipping on my house shoes, I grabbed my robe, tied it, and headed to the door. Normally, I let Kobe out into the fenced-in backyard. But first, I wanted to check my porch to ensure I didn't have any packages from last night that may have been delivered late. It was the Christmas season, and I had been doing a lot of shopping.

I opened the door just to take a quick peek, and Kobe ran right out from under me.

"Come back here, Kobe!" I ran out the door, trying to catch my dog, who had a good time running through the snow. The fluffy pink slippers I had on were getting wet and proving useless in moving me through the snow. By the time I got down my front stairs, Kobe had darted across the street and through the neighbor's yard.

"Aaaahh," I yelled.

At my wits end, I knew I had to run back into the house and get some real shoes. As soon as I hit the porch, the mailman was coming through the front yard with a bunch of parcels.

"Morning," the postman uttered.

"Good morning," I answered back, trying to decide if I needed to bring the packages inside or stick with my mission to grab my tennis shoes.

"I see you have a lot of packages here. Are

you getting ready for Christmas?" The mailman inquired.

"Uh yeah," I answered, preoccupied. I could tell the mailman was put off at my abrasiveness. I was not my usual happy-go-lucky self.

"I'm sorry. It's just that I lost my dog. He ran off," I answered. The mailman placed the last of the parcels on my porch.

"Well, I did see a little dog about two streets over. Is he brown?" He asked.

"Yes, a little light brown on top of his head."

"Let me put my bag in my vehicle, and I will run back over that way and see if I can find him for you."

"That would be amazing. Thank you, I'm going to run inside and grab some real shoes," I yelled out to the mailman who'd joined my mission.

Realizing I probably looked pretty crazy, I tried to run my hand across my unruly hair and remove the morning crust from my eyes. Which I knew wasn't much help since my dog hadn't even let me brush my teeth before rushing out the front door.

Abandoning my once fluffy house shoes

at the door, I'd leave the front door open in case Kobe decided to come back on his own. Inside, I ran to my room to grab a new pair of socks and a pair of tennis shoes. I hurried and put them on, grabbed my keys, and ran back outside.

I rushed down the second set of stairs to the sidewalk and attempted to follow the mailman over to the next block. He was moving much faster than I was as he was dressed for the weather.

"Kobe," I yelled out several times, hoping he would hear me and come back. The mailman moved out of my line of vision. I moved along faster. When I turned the corner, the mailman was gone, and Kobe was nowhere to be found.

My heart sank.

I didn't know what I'd do without my little dog. Exasperated, I was almost ready to give up and turn back.

"I got him," the mailman called out.

"Oh my gosh, thank you," I yelled out, giggling. I held my arms out for Kobe. I couldn't see much. The snowfall was now blinding. He had the dog tucked under his arms. I stood there waiting for them to get closer to me. However, when they reached me, the dog he had wasn't Kobe.

"Oh no, this isn't Kobe," my smile quickly faded.

"Shit, let me take him back. Don't worry. I'll keep looking," he took off running.

"I'm going to get my car," I yelled out. By this time, big tears sat on the rims of my eyes. The snow was getting deeper fast.

Back in front of my house, I hopped in my car and started the window wipers so I could see. Driving slowly, I rolled the two front windows down since I hadn't had time to brush the snow off them. I perused the block slowly, hoping to see Kobe sitting in someone's yard.

"Kobe," I yelled out again, praying he would hear me. I rounded the block, this time seeing Mr. Postman walking. I pulled up to him.

"No luck?" I asked.

"Nah, and I gotta get back to work, but I will keep an eye out for him. I only have two more relays before my break. I'll use my break to walk the neighborhood again," he volunteered.

"You don't have to use up your break

time. I'll drive around. I may have to get some flyers made up, but I'm praying Kobe will come back. Can I give you a ride to your vehicle?" I offered.

"No thanks, I'm not allowed," he answered before taking off in a slow jog.

I drove around for another thirty minutes, and Kobe was nowhere to be found. Giving up, I headed home. I would stop by Staples to have some flyers made up to hang in the neighborhood on my way to work.

Mr. Postman was sitting in a chair on my porch when I pulled up in front of my house. He wasn't holding anything, and Kobe was nowhere around him.

I swallowed the despair in my throat.

I stepped out of my vehicle and headed to the porch. Mr. Postman stood up to greet me.

Suddenly unable to control my tears, I blurted out.

"I couldn't find him."

"No, wait," Mr. Postman called out. He held his arm out in a stop motion.

But it was too late tears poured uncontrollably from my eyes.

Kobe's head popped up out of Mr. Postman's mailbag.

"Oh my God, you scared me to death." I slipped on my stairs, trying to get to him. "Don't ever do that again." Kobe was shivering. He wasn't used to being out in the elements for long periods.

"Yeah, he was freezing, so I stuck him in my bag to warm him up," he said.

"Thank you so much. How can I ever repay you?" I repeated to the mailman.

"Don't worry about it. You don't have to repay me. Us mail carriers run into stray dogs all the time," he said. "What's your name anyway?"

"My name is Blake, Blake Carrington," I answered. "And yours?"

"Naveed Peace," he answered.

"Nice name," I commented.

"Thank you," Naveed answered.

As Naveed opened my screen door, I attempted to spruce up my appearance again.

"I'm sorry. I know I'm looking crazy. I just got out of bed because Kobe had to pee," I shrugged.

"No worries, I understand, although I

AMBER GHE

think you're sexy despite the crust in your eyes," Naveed joked, causing me to blush.

"Oh, so you have jokes this morning?" We laughed.

Suddenly realizing I had several packages waiting on me to lug inside, I pushed Kobe through the front door and gathered a few in my arms.

"You know I can help with that."

Naveed sat the packages inside my front door. "Looks like you need to stay off the home shopping channel," he joked.

"Well, I would, but these packages are for Christmas," I answered.

"I see. You must have a big family?" Naveed inquired.

"Not too big, we just really have a good time celebrating the holidays. What about you?" I asked.

"Not so much. I'll probably end up drinking a beer and watching the game alone." Naveed had gone silent. "Well, I'm running behind on my route. I guess I better get a move on."

"Yes, I'm sure you need to get moving. Thank you again so much for helping me out.

I greatly appreciate you." I opened my door and stepped inside, Kobe running up to me.

"You're welcome," Naveed replied as he headed down the stairs.

I stood there and stared at him as he headed towards his vehicle, grabbed his mailbag, and proceeded to his route.

He was a nice-looking man. I'd never really paid much attention before today, but that smile and those pretty teeth had me doing a double-take.

Using my foot, I moved the packages out of the way to close the door and kicked off my now wet tennis shoes. It was time to get the morning started the way it was supposed to have happened in the first place.

My hands were freezing. I headed to the kitchen and turned on lukewarm water, allowing it to soothe my frigid fingers. If what just happened was any indication of how my day would be, I could already tell it was going to be a long one. Moving quickly to start a pot of coffee, I had to make up for lost time.

A half-hour later, I was stepping into warm tights, pulling my dress down, and tugging at my cozy Ugg boots. I pulled on a Blazer and made sure to pull a few curls from around my bun in the front and back. Next, I swiped rouge red lipstick across my lips to finish my look.

This time of the year was so nostalgic for me. Glancing into the other room at the pile of boxes and bags that were taking over a corner in my living room, I knew I had a lot of work to do. My tree was a gorgeous seven-foot spruce. Still, like a big kid, I couldn't wait for the holidays. I couldn't wait for the sweet fragrance of pies baking, the trimmings, and the conversation.

After pouring a mug of hot coffee, I sat down and opened my cell phone to scroll social media. Everyone was showing off their Christmas trees, lights, and decorations.

Huge snowflakes falling outside the window caught my attention. It was so beautiful and would have been even more so if I hadn't had to go out in it. But being a business owner had its perks. I glanced at my watch and realized it was time for me to get going. I had to go in and audit the holiday inventory. Before leaving, I made sure Kobe had his meal and added fresh drinking water to his bowl. I threw on my coat and stepped out the front door.

Driving over several blocks, Naveed was still trekking through the snow delivering mail in this cold, harsh weather. The snow had to be several inches thick. It would be my intention to do something to thank him for finding Kobe for me this morning, but what?

Even though I was excited about the holidays, I realized I was alone. It crossed my mind again how handsome he was, but my mother would flip if I dated a mailman. I hated that Blue-collar workers were frowned upon by my bougee parents, who wanted my sisters and me to marry attorneys or doctors.

CHAPTER 2
NAVEED

"FUCK!"

I was way behind on my route after helping that lady find her dog. I swear every other day, somebody's dog was loose. At least he wasn't a vicious dog because Lord knows I'd been attacked one too many times. Hell, it was already cold out here, not to mention the snow falling made my workday even longer.

Blake was beautiful, and for a split second, I wondered what it would be like being with someone like her. I swear her running around in those frou-frou house shoes told me she had no clue what it was like to be out in these streets in this pressing cold and snow. She'd never give me a chance, though. I could tell by the beautiful interior of her home when I set the packages inside the door that she and I were on different wavelengths.

Delivering my last parcel for the street, I headed back to the LLV, (my work truck,) set my bag inside the back, and hopped in. I stayed there for a minute, letting the engine run. I needed some heat. My toes were frozen, and I could barely feel the tips of my fingers.

My stomach growling caught my attention. I would stop at McDonald's to grab a sandwich and a hot coffee before continuing my route. Sitting by the window inside the restaurant to people watch. It was Saturday. There were a lot of families walking around downtown shopping and doing things for the holiday. In my opinion, that would never be my life, because number one, I worked long, grueling hours. Number two, I had no family so, it would just be me watching others enjoy the holiday, which I hated.

After lunch, it was my intention to work hard to make up for the lost time this morning. Only, when I got back to the station, I was given more mail. Pissed, I headed back out to deliver the extra mail. I grabbed my bag and stacked a bundle of mail on my arm. Walking down the street and approaching each mailbox, I shoved Christmas card after Christmas card into the different mailboxes. Delivering mail this time of year sucked. Looking at all these Christmas cards, holiday stamps, and fancy handwriting ruined my mood. Not to mention the decorations on the houses and Santa Claus sitting in the yard were enough to make anyone slit their wrists. Sure, it was job security. But delivering mail this time of year could be exhausting.

This time approaching an apartment complex, I opened the big metal box with about twenty mailboxes inside, and I began to fill them when I was interrupted.

"Do you have my check? I'm in apartment 205?" A woman with a bonnet on her head asked.

"Ma'am, you have to give me time to load the mailboxes," I answered.

"I don't see why you can't just give me my mail?" The woman snapped.

See, this is why I don't have the patience for

this, I thought. Blocking the woman out of my mind, she continued standing over my shoulder. It was all I could do. Just so happened, her box was the last one I filled. Grabbing the big door, I swung it shut and locked the mailboxes.

"That's wrong. You could have let me get my mail out of the box before you shut the door." the woman fumed.

"It's against policy, ma'am. You could be anybody going in anybody's mailbox. For your safety, you have to have a key to get into your mailbox." I headed back to my truck. I was over it.

Back at the station, ready to leave for the day, I grabbed my timecard.

"Peace, I need you to deliver the rest of this route. I'm sorry, I hate to have to do this to you because I know it's cold out there, but we gotta get this mail delivered," my boss explained. "Harris went home early."

"Oh man, I'm tired. I just want to go home and lay down," I complained.

"I know, man, but we gotta get this delivered," my boss repeated.

I groaned before grabbing the white plastic tote. One filled with mail and another one filled with parcels and went back to the main strip where I'd just had lunch. I got out of my truck and headed to the back. Almost all of them had the 'So Clutch' labels on them, which happened to be the boutique across the street. I stacked the totes and headed that way. The ringing of a little bell caught my attention when I opened the door.

"Oh, hey. Naveed, right? I've never seen you deliver over here before. Are you following me?" She flirted.

It was her, the beautiful woman from this morning. Suddenly, I wasn't upset about the extra route I was given.

"Hey Blake," I answered, lugging the totes through the door.

"You remembered my name," she exclaimed.

"Of course, I remember. How could I forget the woman running through the snow in fluffy pink house shoes, and robe, with crust in her eyes," I joked.

"Running, I almost broke my neck." she professed. "I'm so embarrassed."

"Nah, I'm just joking, but you really should do something about the pile of snow on your stairs," I replied, entering further into the boutique. "The regular carrier on this route went home early, so I had to pick up some extra hours," I explained. "So, this is where you work, huh?"

"Yes, I own this store," Blake looked around as if giving me a mini-tour of the place.

"'So-Clutch,' huh, what does that mean?" I asked, referring to the name of her store.

"Handbags, often referred to as clutch's, are my specialty. I also sell some other exclusive items like shoes, scarves, capes, and things like that," Blake explained.

I shook my head up and down. "That's cool."

Lugging the tote of parcels up to the counter where she was standing, I joked around, making Blake believe they were extremely heavy.

"Shopping again, I see," I joked.

"Yeah, you've caught me. I am guilty of shopping too much," Blake smiled and started to unpack the parcels from the tote.

"Let me help you with that."

We both started pulling packages out of the totes and accidentally brushed hands.

We smiled at each other. Staring a moment too long, things got a little awkward, but we kept unpacking the packages.

"You know I'm starting to think running into you twice today means something. Would you like to go for some coffee or something when you get off?" I asked.

"Well, I?" she stumbled over her words.

"Oh, that was dumb. Never mind, I shook my head, trying to shake the thought off.

"No, wait, I would like to. I'm sorry I was just a little tongue-tied. It's been a while since anyone's asked me on a date," Blake smiled.

"Well, don't think of it as a date. Let's just say we're going out for a beverage, okay?" I commented.

"Well, I get off late, so how about coffee and a pastry tomorrow on Sunday? Would that work for you?" She asked.

"Yeah, that would work. How about eleven? We can meet at the coffee shop across the street. Is that cool?"

"That would be wonderful," Blake replied.

A smile graced my face as I realized I had asked Blake out for coffee. Once we emptied the totes, I grabbed them and headed back to my truck. Digging into another tote, I grabbed two big handfuls of mail, placed the one in my bag, and put the other on my arm. Time was flying by, and I had finished delivering all of the mail from the second route before I knew it.

Navigating the post office's LLV back to the station, I prayed I would not be given any more mail to deliver. Carrying the totes back inside, I sat them down next to the casing station.

"Well, you're back fast," my supervisor commented.

"Yeah, and I do not want any more mail, thank you," I commented.

"Nah, that's it for today. I'll see you next week," my supervisor turned around to complete whatever he was working on. Grabbing my timecard, I swiped it and headed out the door.

Anxious to head home, I opened the door and climbed inside my car. I knew I was on some bullshit. I couldn't figure out why I asked Blake out because it was inevitable that she would leave like all the others. After this long week, I was in desperate need of rest and relaxation. I pulled off all of my wet, cold clothes and dropped them in the washer when I got home. I took a hot shower, grabbed some leftovers from the fridge, a beer, and headed to the TV.

CHAPTER 3
BLAKE

A DISTINCT SMIRK SAT ON MY FACE AS I WATCHED Naveed leave the boutique. I closed my eyes, trying to envision myself with a man that I actually liked, not some prearranged debacle. "*Pull it together. It's just coffee,*" I thought.

My sister came out of the backroom.

"Did you say something?" Brielle asked.

Smiling, I said. "No, not at all," I lied.

"We got some new inventory," my sister Brielle noted, pulling packing paper off a box.

"Yes, I'm so excited! Look at these sexy handbags from the New York Fashion Week show." The selection of handbags had been a no-brainer, I confirmed once I began opening the packages that Naveed dropped off to me.

"Girl, when are you going to clean this place? You got packages everywhere. The customers won't even be able to look at anything," my sister chastised.

"Feel free to help out. I mean, this is your place of employment," Brielle smirked.

"Ooh, this is so cute," I gushed after pulling the box's contents out.

Opening the packages, I admired all of the beautiful selections I picked out.

"You gotta admit I have good taste when it comes to this kind of stuff."

I placed shoes and handbags together that complimented each other for the photoshoot.

"Now that is to die for," Brielle walked over to admire the new handbag. "Sometimes I feel like I spend my whole paycheck on your inventory," she frowned.

"As long as I'm making sales, I'm doing what I set out to do," I joked.

"Yes, at my expense," Brielle laughed. "But seriously, Blake, you need to get a handle on this shopping. You seriously go crazy this time of year. Why don't you sell some of the stuff you have before buying new inventory?"

I blew out air. "You're right, but I can't help it. I'm addicted to the smell of new inventory." I laughed, "I like to have the freshest new stuff available, but I should get rid of some of this old stuff."

Brielle gave me a blank stare, and I blinked several times with my lips pressed to keep from speaking out.

I picked up a bag of scarves and a pair of shoes and put them on display. They looked perfect together. Grabbing my iPhone, I would snap a few shots to post to my online boutique. I rearranged them and took a few more photos.

My boutique was designed to look like you were in someone's living room. The walls were smoked gray, which complimented the pink carpet and black and pink couches.

The door swung open, causing the little bell to ring.

"Hello, what can I do for you today?" I called out to the women who entered.

"Hi," the cheerful lady called out. Her

friend smiled. "We came in to see if you had any new merchandise," the first lady said.

"See, I told you," I said over my shoulder to my sister. "You're in luck. I just received some new stuff from Fashion Week in New York," I stated proudly.

"Oh my gosh, I can't wait to see," the second lady expressed. Both headed my way, smiling from ear to ear. I could tell they were ready to do some damage, and I was here for the shenanigans. I pointed to the displays in front of me. I could take pictures later.

"Ladies, I'm telling you this stuff was hot in New York, and it sold like hotcakes," I stood to the side, giving them time to look things over. They were squealing and picking up items. Noticing they were indecisive, it was time for me to work my magic.

"Are you looking for something for work or play?" I asked.

"Well, we're going on a cruise, so we're trying to find some accessories to wear to the captain's ball," the first lady explained.

"Then I have just the thing for you." I grabbed a box that I had behind the counter and pulled out a sexy sparkly heel with a matching handbag. "Now, I almost kept this for myself, but this is definitely something you would wear to a Captain's ball, ladies. I know where I can get another one, so if you like this, I can give you the hookup," I whispered even though no one else was around.

"Oh my God, Kelly, that would look so good with your dress," the first girl said to the second.

"You're right it would. I'll take it. I need shoes in size seven, please." I headed to the back to grab the shoe in a seven. While I was back there, I found another bag to show them. It was bronze with a gold chain and matching heels. I grabbed it to show the other lady. When I went back out, I laid it on the counter.

"Ladies, I was going to put this out for New Year's Eve, but it sounds like you need this item for your cruise." I smiled when the first girl picked it up.

"You must have read my mind that this would go so well with my dress." Both ladies squealed as they ran over to the mirror, posing with their handbags and shoes.

"So good, right?" She said to the second lady.

"Oh my God, yes," the first lady exclaimed. Both ladies ran back to the counter with their items and credit cards in hand. I wrapped their items by hand and placed them in big shopping bags, along with the shoes. Once the ladies headed towards the door, I eyed my sister.

"I told you, girl," I smiled.

"Yeah, you were right," Brielle waved me off.

As my customers were leaving, my mother and my other sister Bailey entered the boutique. Both of them were dressed to kill as always. Bailey was the younger prototype of my mother in more ways than one.

"Hey, Mom, hey Bailey, you guys look beautiful. Where are you going?" I asked.

"Oh, we're just going to have dinner over at Christopher Soho's. We thought we'd stop by and see if you ladies wanted to join us?" My mother informed me.

"Mom, I don't have any workers today, so I can't go. I have to tend to the boutique."

I was hungry, too. "Maybe you could bring me back carryout?" I asked.

"I want to go," my sister Brielle said, jumping up to go grab her stuff. "You got this, don't you, Blake? I mean, you don't have any customers right now, so you should be okay."

"You are the owner of the shop. You can do what you want to do," my mother informed.

"You know what, Mom, you're right. I'll just put an out-to-lunch sign on the door. I'll stay out for about an hour and come back," I said, gathering my jacket and purse. We all left the boutique, and I locked the door behind me.

"I'll take my car so that way I can get back when I'm ready," I suggested. "Brielle, you can come back to work with me when you get finished."

Minutes later, we pulled up to Christopher Soho's and walked inside. The restaurant was polished and sophisticated, the atmosphere full of energy. Not to mention the Christmas decorations were on point.

It was around happy hour, so the crowd was bustling. We followed the waiter to the table after my mother said she had a reservation for the Carrington party. After being seated comfortably in our booth, we ordered hors d'oeuvres and drinks while waiting for our meals to arrive.

"So, do any of you have dates for Christmas dinner?'' My mother inquired, eyeing each of us.

"I swear, mom, you act like you're trying to marry us off or something," I said before my sisters, and I cringed.

"I'm just trying to prepare enough food for everyone," my mother purred.

"I have a date," my sister Bailey informed.

"I have a date, too, Mom," Brielle added.

"No, I don't have a date, but I will be there, ready to help prepare food if you need me to." I smiled at my mom, hoping my answer was to her liking.

"You know my friend Marge has a charming son your age, and I believe you two would be a nice fit for each other. Oh, and did I mention he's a doctor?" Mother picked up her fork and inspected it. I smirked.

"Mom, I don't need you to fix me up. I mean, if it's dire that I bring someone, I can always call up one of my exes," I joked. Mother rolled her eyes at me. The waiter served our meals, and we dug in.

CHAPTER 4
NAVEED

I was relieved to be home after getting off work. Even though I was exhausted, thinking about Blake caused me to lick my lips. The fact that I would see her again tomorrow had me distracted like a mug.

Remembering the massive mound of curls bouncing around her face this morning had me wondering what my motives were. Lord, I pray this hot water gives me life. And it did prove to give me a second wind. After my hot shower, I grabbed a beer, pulled some takeout out of the refrigerator, and threw it in the microwave. My lazy boy chair was calling my name.

Pushing the Chinese leftovers aside, I took a nice long gulp of the beer. I picked up the remote control and turned on the TV. The commercials had been playing, so I hadn't realized Family Feud was the featured show. I groaned. I immediately grabbed the remote control to change the channel. I couldn't stand those family game shows. Effectively turning on ESPN to watch some sports, I was able to relax. This was more my speed, something that didn't have anything to do with your typical 'Leave it to Beaver' family.

All of that stuff reminded me of my grandmother. She had to watch her game shows in the morning and her soap operas in the afternoon. I was always stuck watching that stuff with her, never getting to watch cartoons.

I always wondered what it would be like to have a doting mom or father to play sports with. I was that boy stuck under his grandmother's wing going to bingo. If I wanted to play sports, I had to do it on my own accord. Because my grandmother wasn't going to get me the equipment to do anything or support me in those endeavors. Despite all of that, I was a survivor and down for the cause.

The next day I woke up feeling refreshed and ready to do something different. Dressing in casual khakis and a sweater, I splashed on my favorite cologne. My mind drifted once again to my grandmother. I wondered if she would have approved of Blake?

I headed over to the 'Coffee Spot,' where we agreed to meet. Once inside, I realized Blake had beat me there. Peering at my watch and confirming that I was on time, I headed to the table where Blake was sitting. Her full lips coated in a subtle gloss and eyelashes were the only indication she had on makeup.

"Hi, I hope you weren't waiting long?" I commented.

"No, not at all. I'm an early riser, so I decided to stop in and peruse social media a bit on my phone while waiting for you," Blake explained.

"What can I get you?" I offered.

"I think I'll take a pumpkin spice latte with an extra shot of espresso."

Blake picked up her phone and started scrolling again. I stepped away to order the coffees. I also picked up a couple of pastries.

Anxious to get back to the table and her fucking beautiful smile, the attendant called my number. I grabbed the tray, headed back to the table, and sat down.

"You look beautiful today," I complimented. She gave me a sexy smirk.

"Thanks. You look like a different person without your uniform," Blake giggled.

"Does that mean I should have worn my uniform? Are you one of those girls who likes a man in uniform?" I joked.

Blake laughed. "Ah, I see you have a sense of humor."

"I try."

Blake picked up her coffee, taking a sip. "I can imagine business for the post office is pretty grueling this time of the year, huh?" she asked.

"Grueling is an understatement when it comes to the post office during Christmas. I hate this time of year."

"Wait, you hate this time of the year because you're busy at work, or you hate this time of the year?" She asked.

"I just think it's overrated. Christmas is too commercialized. All these people running out spending hundreds of dollars on toys just doesn't seem right," I clarified.

"Me, on the other hand, I love Christmas. I love everything about Christmas. Christmas can be a fun time of the year. I love making other people happy," Blake smiled.

I smiled back. However, I could tell this was something we just didn't see eye-to-eye on.

"I can imagine business is pretty good for you this time of the year, is that correct?" I asked, trying to shift the tone of the conversation.

"Yes, as a matter of fact, I seem to do pretty well year-round. There's always something going on that a woman could use a new handbag or shoes." Blake stopped talking to sip her coffee. I gulped mine as well. "Yeah, we always seem to find an occasion to go shopping," Blake laughed.

"Tell me a little bit about yourself. Are you from Columbus?" I asked.

"Yes, I am. I've been here my whole life. What about you?" She asked.

"I'm actually from Springfield, Ohio," I noted.

"Oh, I've never been to Springfield. Where is it?" Blake questioned.

"It's about 30 minutes outside of Columbus, a little town where everybody knows everybody. Not much to write home about," I remarked.

"Well, we have a pretty big family here in Columbus. I have two sisters, a slew of aunts and uncles and cousins. Yeah, we do it up big for everything, barbecues parties, yeah, we show out. I'll have to invite you to one of our cookouts. It's crazy how much food there is when we have one of our parties," Blake advised.

"I'd love to come to one of your cookouts," I acknowledged.

"Do you have any family here?" She questioned.

"No, I don't. My grandmother raised me, and when she passed away, I left Springfield. I'm just kind of hanging out here and working. I don't have much of a life at this point."

My story sounded pretty pitiful, and if I were Blake, I wouldn't be somebody I'd be interested in hanging out with again. Uncomfortable with the conversation, I shifted in my seat and wondered if I should find an excuse to get out of this.

"Naveed, what are your aspirations in life? Do you plan on working for the post office long-term?" Blake asked.

I lifted an eyebrow, taking a beat to sip my coffee. "No one's ever asked me that before. Is there something wrong with working for the post office long term?"

"Not at all," Blake blushed. "I was just wondering."

Not wanting her to feel too uncomfortable, I lightened my tone. "I'd been kind of winging it, never giving it much thought. But no, I don't aspire to work for the Post Office for the rest of my life. However, I've never figured out anything else I could do. You know, maybe I'll go home and put some thought into that question and get back to you."

"That would be awesome. I think you should do that. Like for me, yeah, I have a boutique, but I aspire to have a chain of boutiques, you know, expand to other cities, maybe even other countries. I would be big like Louis Vuitton or Gucci one day and put my own products out," Blake explained.

I shook my head. "You know I could totally see that happening for you. It's amazing you have big dreams as a business owner. You're inspiring me to reflect on my own situation," I contemplated. Blake's energy was bond and made me feel good, like I wanted to be better.

"Naveed, I've had an amazing time with you, but I do have some other appointments that I need to get to today."

Blake gathered her things.

"You know if I do my homework, I would have to get back with you so I can tell you what I've come up with," I advised.

"That would be amazing, Naveed. I would love to hear what you come up with." Blake passed me her phone. "Type your number in here, please." I followed her command and hit the send button, ensuring that the call came to my phone, prompting me to have her number as well.

"Okay, I'll give you a call soon."

I stood up, put my coat on, and when she stood up, I helped Blake into her jacket, and walked her to her car. I wanted to make sure she got off safely.

"Hey, be careful out on these roads. They

can be quite slippery in this weather," I advised.

"I will. You too, and thanks again, Naveed. I enjoyed myself," Blake pulled out in her cute SUV before I headed to my Lexus.

CHAPTER 5
BLAKE

THERE WAS SORT OF A MYSTERY TO NAVEED, almost as if he were hiding himself from me. I pulled off from the restaurant and headed over to the boutique. Because deliveries were non-stop this time of year, I was trying to get on top of things.

"Good morning. How are you, sis?" Brielle chirped.

"I'm good. I stopped off for coffee this morning, so I'm feeling pretty good right now," I grinned.

"Oh, did you bring me a cup?" My sister looked around.

"Oh my gosh, I'm sorry. I didn't even

think to grab you a cup. I had somewhat of a date this morning."

Brielle's eyes lit up in response to my comment.

"Wait, what did you say? You had a date?" My sister smirked.

"Don't get your panties all in a bunch. It was just coffee, nothing big," I assured, hoping she wouldn't press for more information.

"I hope you don't think that I'm just going to settle for, '*Oh, it was just coffee?*' I need details. Who is this mystery guy?" Just as I knew she would, Brielle pressed for more information.

"Girl, stop making this into more than what it is." I opened another package pulling out a cute pair of strappy heels. "Oh, these are so cute," I grinned, hoping to sway her attention to something else.

"Those are cute. However, don't try to get off topic right now," Brielle insisted.

"Okay, so I know you're going to judge me, but it's the mailman that delivered the packages yesterday. We met for coffee and conversation. Nothing big, okay?" I confided.

"You know Mom would freak out if she knew I went on a date with the mailman."

"I don't see anything wrong with it as long as he's a nice guy," Brielle defended.

"That's how I feel about it; however, I don't think it will go anywhere. We seem to be in two different universes. Number one, he doesn't even like Christmas, and you know how I feel about Christmas," I noted.

"God, forbid he doesn't like Christmas. Is that really a deal-breaker for you?" My sister declared.

It did sound crazy the way she made it sound. I shrugged and continued to open the packages pulling out more handbags and matching shoes. I lined them up on the countertop for photos. This was the fun part, arranging everything for pictures and then uploading it on the website later. I had to do it all. I wore all the hats in my business, marketing, promotion, and supervisor. I did it all.

Business was good but not that good. I needed a team of people to work for me. All of this kept me too busy, but that was the part that I enjoyed.

"Girl, you are not even going to put these

on the floor because I got to have these shoes," Brielle shrieked.

"Only if you pay for them, and you can't hide stuff in the backroom indefinitely," I insisted.

Brielle smirked.

Later, after taking inventory and photos to upload to my website, I was ready to call it an evening. It was Sunday, and I usually closed a little earlier than normal. Hugging my sister, I told her I would see her later. I headed home. My best friend Tracy was going to come by and have dinner with me.

This evening was going to be laid back. I stopped by the grocery store to grab a bottle of wine also grabbing a package of pasta, some sauce, and some grilled chicken from the deli.

Thirty minutes later, I arrived home to Kobe greeting me.

"Hey, baby," I called out to my cute little Pomeranian. Did you miss Mommy?" Yes, I am a dog mom, don't judge.

Heading to the kitchen to set my packages down. I opened the back door so Kobe could go outside to relieve himself and come right back. I stood at the door, knowing he would only be out there long enough to do his duty. When he arrived on the back porch, he shook off the snow and proceeded into the house. I had a rug at the back door where he wiped his feet.

"Come on," I said, heading back into the kitchen to wash my hands and prepare the Chicken Alfredo.

The blare of the doorbell snatched me out of my thoughts.

Swinging the door open, I greeted my best friend. "Hey, girl, I missed you. How are you doing?" I asked, giving Tracy a big hug.

"Hey, Blake. I feel like I haven't seen you in forever. We've both been so busy. You know my job is getting to me. Girl, they are working me to death. They need to go on and hire some more people," Tracy declared.

"I feel you on that. Maybe you should quit your job and come work at the boutique," I joked, knowing she would never leave her job. It was fulfilling to her. "Hey, come on in here and get some wine," I suggested.

"Yes, you knew what I was thinking."

Tracy followed me into the kitchen,

where I grabbed two wine glasses out of the cabinet and set them on the island.

"Oh, you got my favorite, the blueberry wine from Cooper Hawk," Tracy pointed out.

"Girl, you know I had to get this. It's so delicious. Dinner is almost ready. Let me just go ahead and throw the French bread in the oven. It should only take it about five minutes to heat up." I explained. "Come on, let's sit down at the table. I didn't get to tell you. I went out for coffee this morning with a guy," I blushed.

"What?" Tracy's brow dipped in confusion. "So, I know we haven't talked in a minute, but it hasn't been that long that you couldn't tell me you were going out on a date," Tracy pursed her lips together.

"I know, but It just kind of happened spur of the moment. We went out for coffee. The conversation was decent. But I'm not sure If we meshed, though. His energy was weird at times. For instance, he doesn't seem too keen on Christmas, and you know, that's like my favorite time of the year," I explained.

Tracy shook her head. "So, what did you think of him other than that? Is he handsome?" Tracy was asking questions so fast I could barely keep up.

"He's very handsome—brown skin, full beard. But there's one thing that I have to tell you." I waited to gauge Tracy's expression to see how she was going to handle the next piece of information. "Naveed, that's his name... is a mail carrier."

"So, he's working, isn't he? I know a lot of women who end up with men who won't even get up and go to work every day," she declared.

"I know. I don't mean to be judgmental, but you know my family is going to trip. Like my mom thinks I should be married to a doctor or something crazy," I told her, blowing out air.

"Well, I refuse to believe that you don't mesh with him just because he doesn't care for Christmas, I mean. I know you're not that shallow. Girl, you need to get to know him and see if you like him as a person. Not to mention getting rid of those dusty ass cobwebs between your legs," Tracy laughed.

"Oooh, no, you didn't," I laughed.

Tracy was right. I really should just get to know him as a friend first, with no expectations, and see if it could lead to anything. I mean, I definitely thought he was handsome.

"I just don't know If I'm ready?" I shrugged.

"Ready for what? Companionship, love, commitment, and letting that Mandingo rock your world?" Tracy laughed and rolled her eyes at me.

"In light of the evidence you have pointed out, I guess that makes sense." I let out a dry laugh. "I think I will try to get to know him as a friend and see what direction things might lead. Still, I'm scared to see what my mom's going to say when she finds out. You know she's all about status." I did air quotes with my hands.

Tracy and I talked into the wee hours of the evening. We had a good time together. It had been a while since we hung out like this, drinking wine, dancing, and telling stories.

"Blake, I should get home. You know I have to be up early in the morning. These students aren't going to teach themselves, unfortunately," she acknowledged.

"I hear you, girl. Yeah, it's time I get a little rest, too."

"Okay, well, think about what I said. I

believe you should, you know, at least go out again," Tracy reminded me.

"I'm going to take you up on your advice," I remarked as Tracy and I walked to the front door. When we reached the door, she zipped up her coat and put on her gloves.

"Hey, call me when you get home, okay? I want to make sure you get home safely."

I opened the door noticing Naveed grabbing a tote of parcels out of the back of his truck.

"Oh, look Tracy, this is him now," I said.

"Poor thing out here delivering on Sunday evening in this weather," she said before looking out the door. "Oooh he is cute." Tracy slapped me on the arm.

"I told you." I laughed.

CHAPTER 6
NAVEED

BACK IN BLAKE'S NEIGHBORHOOD, I PARKED AE OUT two blocks away from where she lived and began dropping parcels on people's porches.

My mind kept reverting back to my efforts to remain upbeat during our coffee date this morning. Yet, at times, I couldn't hide the fact that I was a moody mess. She gave me the impression that today didn't go very well, grilling me about my profession and shit. I didn't blame her. Hell, if I was a successful business owner, I wouldn't be looking to build a life with a mail carrier either. But it was all good. It came with the job description.

After that, I pulled up to my house and

headed inside. I swear, as soon as I shut the door, my boss was calling.

"Yeah," I answered.

"Peace, we need you in here to work on this Amazon Prime. We're down four routes," my boss informed me.

"Oh man, you gotta be kidding me," I huffed.

"My hands are tied. I need you in here today," my boss reiterated.

Knowing I didn't have any other plans, I gave in.

I'll be there. Give me a few to get changed." I ended the call, not wanting to hear anything else he had to say.

My bed beckoned me like a hot date as I headed towards my room. I wanted to jump in so bad and get some more sleep; however, it was not written in my destiny today. So, instead, I threw on a clean uniform and a second pair of socks. Knowing I would be out in that snow, I added a sweatshirt, coat, and gloves, all the things I needed to keep myself warm out on my route.

A half an hour later, I entered the station.

My boss smiled too hard at me, making me suspect. "Peace, I'm so glad you made it.

Man, I just need you to run your regular route, except there will only be the Amazon packages today," my boss headed back to his office.

With my gloves tucked under my arm, I grabbed the keys to my vehicle and opened the back. I pretty much knew I could knock these parcels down in a couple of hours, and I would be back home in no time drinking a beer in my lazy boy watching football. The thought of it caused me to put a little pep in my step along with the coffee I drank earlier.

When it came time to hit Blake's street, I parked in front of her house because I knew she had a lot of packages. I opened the back of my vehicle, grabbed a tote full of parcels because they were all hers, and headed up the first set of stairs. As I reached the second set of stairs to the porch, I slipped and fell.

"Oh shit," I yelled, grabbing my leg. "Damn, it hurts," I grunted.

"What happened? Oh my God, are you alright," Blake hollered out, attempting to run down the stairs.

"No, you need to be careful. You have an ice patch on your stairs. Don't you have some salt or a shovel or something?" I chastised.

"You got us out here delivering all this shit, and you don't even bother to shovel the stairs?" I grunted in pain.

"I'm so sorry. The guy who normally shovels hasn't been around. I don't know why. Here let me help you up." She offered.

"Blake, what happened?" There was another voice that I didn't recognize.

"Tracy, my mailman fell, and I believe he's hurt," Blake yelled. "Can you gather up all the packages that spilled, and I'll try to help Naveed."

Blake reached and attempted to help me up, but something had to be broken. My leg did not feel right, and I couldn't put any pressure on it at all.

"Do you think you can walk?" Blake asked.

"No, it hurts like shit?" I answered.

"Should I call the paramedics?" Blake asked.

"Here's what I need you to do. Go to my vehicle and get my cell phone out of the glove box. Bring it here so I can call my boss and let him know I can't walk."

Blake followed my instructions, bringing me my cell phone. I promptly called my supervisor to let him know I had fallen and was unable to walk.

"I'm on my way. Can you hold on for a few minutes until I get there?" My boss Robert inquired.

"Yeah, I think I can," I responded, knowing we weren't far from the station. Blake and her friend gathered the packages, which were all Blake's anyway, and took them up to her house. I sat there in pain and embarrassment, trying to gather my scruples, when I noticed my boss pulling up.

"Peace, why you out here on this lady's property causing trouble?" My supervisor joked.

"Haha," I muttered, knowing the joke was on me.

"I just got to take a quick safety report, and then I'll get you over to Urgent Care," he stated.

"Can you at least help me get inside the vehicle first? It's cold out here," I added.

"Of course."

Blake and her friend she called Tracy helped me get inside the vehicle.

Groaning, my leg throbbed in pain after

trying to put pressure on my leg. It hurt so damn bad.

"I'll follow you over there," I heard Blake say to my boss. Pulling on the driver's side door, he stepped inside the vehicle. The other mail carrier the supervisor brought with him opened the back of my vehicle to complete the route.

Blake hugged her friend before heading to separate vehicles.

"Let me just get you over here to Urgent Care," my boss said. I was quiet. I really didn't have much to say since my plans to watch the game in my lazy boy were now going to be a thing of the past.

"IT'S BROKEN," THE DOCTOR SHOWED US ON THE X-ray. "You'll need to be off of it for at least four weeks before we can put you in a boot," he explained to me.

"Oh, man, not my best carrier during the Christmas season," my supervisor fussed.

CHAPTER 7
BLAKE

AFTER LOCKING UP MY HOUSE, I HEADED OVER TO Urgent Care to check on Naveed. I felt horrible. I knew those stairs were slippery because I almost fell on them the other day. I pulled up to Urgent Care and headed inside.

"I'm here to check on Naveed Peace," I said to the lady at the front desk.

"Let me check. What's your name?" She asked.

"Blake Carrington," I answered.

She got up and went to the back. I stood there looking around at the waiting room. It wasn't very crowded, which was a good thing. They must have taken him straight back. The lady from the desk returned.

"Follow me," she said.

Following the lady, she took me back to the room where Naveed and his supervisor were.

"Hi," I waved. "Naveed, I hope you don't mind that I'm here. I feel terrible about what happened." I repeated for what felt like the one hundredth time today.

"I'm actually on my way out of here. I gotta get back to the station. Naveed, call me when you're ready to get home. I'll give you a ride." His boss offered.

"I can give him a ride. if that's okay with Naveed?" I suggested.

"That's fine. I don't have a problem with it," Naveed expressed.

The doctor entered the room with supplies to cast his leg.

"Oh, my goodness, it's broken?" I questioned.

"Yes, he has a broken Fibula. On the other hand, that is the smaller bone, which with proper rest will heal pretty fast."

The doctor placed his supplies on the bedside table.

"Yeah, I'll need to be off of it for about four weeks before they can put a boot on it.

This is kind of rough because this is our busy season," Naveed added.

I stood there so ashamed, knowing that I put this man off of his job for so long.

"It sounds like your boss will have to file a claim with my insurance. Hopefully, that will cover your medical expenses and, you know, some of your time off of the job. I don't have a problem with it. I mean, it is my fault."

"We can talk about all of that later," Naveed noted.

The doctor finished wrapping Naveed's cast. They brought him in a pair of crutches and adjusted them to his height.

"We'll write you a script. I know you're in a lot of pain right now. You really shouldn't be by yourself for the first 24 to 48 hours. You'll have a hard time getting around and may be woozy from your pain meds. Is there someone who can help you out?" The doctor insisted.

"I can help him," I volunteered.

"Great, my nurse will be right in with your discharge papers, and then you can be on your way." The doctor cleaned up his supplies and headed out of the room.

"Thank you for telling the doctor you would help me, but I don't need a babysitter," Naveed said.

"Oh no, I took on the request, so I'm going to follow through. It's settled. You'll be staying with me for a couple of days."

"No, it's settled that you'll be staying with me for a couple of days because there's no way I can get up the stairs at your house. That's what got us in this predicament in the first place," Naveed cringed in pain.

"Okay, but you know I'll have to bring Kobe with me," I added.

"Kobe is not a deal-breaker, so bring him with you."

I shrugged. The nurse tapped on the door before entering the room.

"Naveed, here is your script for your pain meds. You're going to take these every four to six hours for the first two days for the pain, and then after that, you can slow down and take them as needed, okay? When you're finished with these, start with ibuprofen for inflammation or Tylenol for pain. If you have any questions feel free to give the doctor a call. Is there anything else I can get for you?"

"No, that's fine."

"Okay, you're free to leave, have a good evening," the nurse added before heading out of the room.

I helped Naveed into his coat. Once he was on his crutches, I stood really close to him like I was going to be able to break his fall if he fell. Helping him out to my vehicle, we headed back to my place.

"I'll grab a few things if you don't mind, and I have to get Kobe."

"Just don't have me sitting out here forever. I really don't feel well," Naveed leaned on the window.

"I'll hurry. Just give me a few minutes."

Heading up the stairs, I took care to ensure I didn't fall either. I ran into the house and grabbed Morton's table salt, and went back outside to sprinkle the stairs. I didn't need anyone else falling who came to deliver packages.

Back inside, I grabbed an overnight bag, packed a couple of outfits and PJ's, comfortable stuff to wear. Then I grabbed Kobe and stuck him in his travel cage. I headed outside to load the bag and Kobe in his cage inside my SUV.

"I'll be right back. I just need to grab his

dog food and lock up," I told Naveed because I knew he was waiting on me.

Leaving a couple of lights on, I moved outside with the bag of dog food, headed over to the driver's side, and jumped in.

"That wasn't long, was it?" I asked.

"No, but we still have to go to the pharmacy," Naveed reminded me.

"Oh yes, we do need to go to the pharmacy." Checking the rearview mirror before pulling out, we headed to CVS.

"Is this where you get your prescription filled?" I asked.

"Yeah, but the one over on Jefferson," Naveed answered.

I kept driving past the one that was near me. It didn't dawn on me that just because he worked over here that he lived this way, I headed over to the CVS on Jefferson. Once there, we pulled into the drive-thru and dropped off the prescription.

"It'll be ready in 15 to 20 minutes," the cashier told us.

"You should probably eat something before you take that medicine. Let's grab some food while we wait," I suggested.

"That sounds good. How about Steak n' Shake?" Naveed suggested.

Pulling back out onto the main road, I headed to Steak n' Shake. Once we grabbed our food, I parked in a space and pulled hand wipes out of my purse. After being in that hospital, I knew we needed to wash our hands before tearing into the hamburgers.

"Hey, I just want to thank you for helping me out. I appreciate it even though you're the cause of me going through this right now," Naveed reminded.

"I know. I feel so bad. I just don't know what else to do to make it up to you."

I turned up the radio, hoping to divert his attention while we ate our hamburgers quietly. Wiping my mouth and throwing the garbage in the bag, I stepped out of the truck to throw everything in the can in the parking lot.

"Your prescription should be ready now," I pulled out of the parking space and headed back over to CVS.

A half-hour later, we were at his house. I ran around to the driver's side, giving Naveed his crutches and following along his side up to his front door.

"Where's the light switch?" I asked, and he pointed. I turned on the light and helped him over to his couch.

"I need to sit here for a second to catch my bearings," Naveed told me.

"Okay, I'm going to grab my things and Kobe out of the car. I'll be right back."

CHAPTER 8
NAVEED

Soon I was all settled in. I did my best to wash up and put on a pair of sweats. I headed straight towards the living room so I could get in my lazy boy. I knew it would be a good way to elevate my leg during my recovery. I got in my chair and laid back.

"Here, I got you a bottle of water so you can take your medicine and go to sleep. If you could just let me know where the sheets and blankets are. I can just kind of lay here on your couch while you rest," she said.

"I pointed down the hall. Blankets are in the linen closet. This is a one-bedroom place, so you won't get lost kitchens over that way," I said sarcastically.

Laying back in my lazy boy, I flipped through channels on the TV while she grabbed blankets and fed Kobe. I don't know what all she was doing. I didn't pay too much attention, groggy now that the medicine was kicking in. Laying there, I had no idea what I was even watching. Feeling comfortable, I kind of liked the fact that she was here with me.

Blake finally appeared to settle down. Scrolling her phone, the light illuminated her face. She was beautiful, were the thoughts I had before dozing off.

That night I dreamed about my grandmother. She was trying to tell me something. I watched her walk over to her jewelry box and pull out a ring.

"That's beautiful," I told her, not thinking too much about why she was showing it to me. So happy to see her face. It had been a long time since I've had any family. I savored these moments even though they weren't real.

Waking up to the smell of breakfast was odd in my home because nobody cooked but me. So, I was quite surprised when Blake entered the room with a tray of pancakes, turkey bacon, orange juice, and fruit. She sat it on the table.

"Good morning. Do you need help getting to the restroom or anything before eating?" She asked.

"No, not yet." The sweet fragrance of maple syrup filled my nostrils.

Blake picked up the tray and set it on my lap. I grabbed the napkin and laid it across my waist, picked up the fork and knife, and began to eat. Blake came back into the room with another tray with food on it for herself and sat on the couch.

"Thank you so much. I can't even tell you the last time someone made breakfast for me," I confessed.

"Oh, it was nothing. Like I said, I feel so responsible, and I know that I need to help you out until you can get back on your feet." Blake reassured me that it wasn't a problem.

"But I can tell you that you know we're going to need to decorate your place. It's so drab here. There's no way you can sit home like this for Christmas and not have any decorations." Blake smiled and continued eating.

"I'm going to run out in a bit and check in

on the boutique. My sister said she would fill in for me. And my other sister Bailey is going to keep Kobe for me while I get you situated," she said.

"Obviously, I'll be here when you get back. My keys are on the table." After that, breakfast and medication sleep should be calling. I'm not going to lie, working hard delivering mail for a long time, I was kind of enjoying this much-needed rest even though I really wasn't the type of man who required a lot of sleep. But being forced into this situation gave me no choice. I guessed I would enjoy it.

Blake gathered her things and left. It was kind of annoying having someone at my house going through my kitchen, my bathroom, and things. Yet, on the other hand, I had been alone so long it felt kind of good to have company.

Turning on ESPN so I could get the update on the sports I missed last night, I lowered my easy boy chair back and closed my eyes. Moments later, I returned to La La Land.

Peppermint invaded my senses. I don't know what was in that last pill, but it felt like

I'd been in a deep sleep for hours. Opening my eyes, my place did not look like my place. It was warm and cozy, lit up with Christmas lights. I blinked hard. This couldn't be right. There was a decorated Christmas tree with lights and stockings hanging off the mantle and...

"I hope you like it. We really needed to brighten the place up around here. There's no way you can heal if you're not feeling comfortable and festive," Blake said.

Honestly irritated because I was forced into this situation, I frowned. "I told you Christmas wasn't my thing," I reiterated.

"I know, but I thought it would make you feel better if somebody did something nice for you. It must be pretty depressing to be down right now, and it's my fault. So, I'm just trying to make it up to you." Blake sounded a little put off by my response.

"I tell you what, I'll leave tomorrow, and when I leave, I'll take my stuff with me," Blake huffed.

Blowing out air, I threw my chair back and closed my eyes. I wasn't sleepy, but I knew I needed to be quiet. Otherwise, things were just going to escalate.

Blake cackled on the phone in the kitchen about how I treated her when she was just trying to cheer me up.

"Girl, his attitude is so stank. Everyone knows how much I love Christmas. He looked around at the decorations like I offended him. It really hurt my feelings," she said to whoever she was talking to on the phone.

"I'm out of here tomorrow, though, I can tell you that much. I'm ready to get back to my holiday the way I like to enjoy it. I mean, yeah, he fell on my property and all. But I didn't have to come over here and help his moody ass out. Hell, I didn't really even know him from a can of fucking paint."

I could only hear half of the conversation. Attempting to tune her out, I turned up the TV. Honestly, she didn't even need to be here another night because I was over the whole situation. Hell, I could get around on them damn crutches. Flipping to the news, they talked about more snow in the forecast how it's been snowing for days.

"We're due to get twenty-two inches within the next few hours. We're suggesting that everybody hunker down and give the trucks a chance to get out and plow the snow. It's deep. It's already piling on top of the snow we already had. If you take a chance to go out, especially in small cars, it's guaranteed you're going to get stuck," The news anchor stated. A commercial about tires played.

"Update, we're now calling it a level three emergency. You are not allowed to be on the streets, only emergency vehicles," the news anchor gave a few more details.

"Naveed, I decided I'm just going to go home. I understand I overstepped my boundaries, and I just don't feel welcomed here," she expressed.

"I'm sorry you feel that way, but unfortunately, you're stuck with me probably until sometime tomorrow. They just announced on the news that there is a level three snow emergency, and you cannot be out on the streets, only emergency vehicles. So, I suggest you get comfortable, get a magazine or something, kick back and enjoy.

CHAPTER 9
BLAKE

THE NERVE OF HIM WITH HIS POMPOUS ASS. Heading towards the window, I looked out. You couldn't see anything. It was a whiteout outside. Pacing the floor, I peered out the window again, probably for the twentieth time in the last twenty minutes since he'd been awake.

I wish he'd hurry up and take another one of those pain pills and fall asleep. I sat down on the couch. I figured if I had to be here, I could at least get some work done, remembering I had all of those photographs in my phone to upload from the boutique. So, I had stuff to do.

About an hour later, I was on the phone

with Tracy again. I moved back into the kitchen. There was very little room for privacy in his house, but I could at least talk without him looking down my throat.

"Hey girl, so what are you going to do?" Tracy asked.

"There's not much I can do at this point but wait until the roads are open, hopefully early tomorrow," I sighed.

Standing up, I moved to the kitchen window. "Doesn't look like it's going to let up anytime soon," shuddering, I caught a cold chill from the window.

"It's actually kind of cool to be snowed in. It hasn't happened since we were kids. It used to be so much fun to have snow days when we were in school," Tracy reminded me.

"That was fun. I really miss those days when we would go outside and make snowmen.

"Girl, if Naveed is that much of a grinch, he'd probably shit his pants if you did that," Tracy laughed.

"Don't give me any ideas. Well, let me get off of here. I guess I'll fix him a Last Supper because I plan on being out of here tomorrow. Then he can take his medicine and go back to sleep. Hopefully, I'll acquire some peace and quiet around here for a few more hours," I laughed.

"Okay, girl, call me back if you get bored. Of course, I'm not going anywhere," Tracy laughed.

"Bye, girl." Hanging up the phone, I got up and washed my hands. Checking the refrigerator to see what I could fix. I pulled out the Eckrich sausage. Next, I grabbed some potatoes sliced them up with onions and green pepper. Adding a little olive oil to the skillet, I seasoned all of the ingredients together. This was an old-school meal. The savory flavors filled the air. We used to make this kind of stuff when I was in college.

I fixed his plate, poured a nice tall glass of orange juice, and headed back into the living room. Naveed was not in his chair. He must have gotten up and gone to the restroom. I sat his plate down on the table and placed the napkin over it to keep it warm.

The crash in the hallway caught my attention. "Naveed, are you okay?" I asked.

"I just got a little woozy, but I think I'm okay," he answered. I immediately moved to help him back to the recliner. Once he was settled, I picked his plate up and handed it to him. He sat the orange juice in the cup holder on the recliner.

"Thank you. I really don't mean to be difficult. It's just that I'm not used to being down like this. I haven't had to rely on anyone since I was a kid. I'm finding out I just don't know how to act," Naveed expressed.

"It's okay. I'm sure breaking your leg and having to be off work during the holidays is rough on you. I mean, I don't want to keep beating a dead horse, but you know I keep saying it's my fault, and that's why I'm here trying to make things right," I explained.

"Blake, I'm not going to sue you if that's what you're thinking," Naveed added.

"No, that's not what I'm thinking at all; however, if you need to in order to pay the doctor's bills and everything, I mean it's understandable. I don't have any malice towards that. I was wrong; I should have shoveled the sidewalk. As a matter of fact, I'll file the claim myself. You deserve to be off work, not running behind on your bills because of me. You didn't ask for that."

Heading to the kitchen, I made myself a plate and returned to the living room.

"That was delicious, is there anymore?" Naveed asked.

"Sure, I'll go get you some," I told him. Minutes later, I returned with his seconds, and he ate the food, which made me feel good. "I see you're getting your appetite. That means you're feeling better," I commented.

"The pain. It isn't as intense as it was. So yeah, I am starting to feel better," he replied.

"That's great."

"Yeah, I don't want to take those narcotics anymore. Think I'll just take regular Tylenol from here on out. I don't like the woozy feeling that the stuff gives me. I'm not a big fan of taking medicine anyway," he said.

"I understand. I don't really take a lot of medication either. Sometimes I'll suffer through headaches even when I know I can take something. Kind of weird, huh?" I shook my head.

"Blake, would you like to watch a movie with me this evening? We might as well try to make the best of things since we're kind of snowed in together. We could act like we're on a date since we can't go anywhere," he suggested.

"As long as you're not going to be mean to me about Christmas. I think I'd like that."

"I promise," he smiled.

"What kind of movie would you like to watch? You know me, I would vote for a cute Christmas movie, but..."

"Okay, don't push it. I'm trying to do better," he smiled.

"Let me take these plates into the kitchen while you check out the guide and tell me what you come up with." I headed into the kitchen, placed the plates in the sink, and started the dishwater. I was ready to knock these dishes out because I was not the type to leave a kitchen dirty.

When I headed back into the living room, Naveed had moved from the recliner to the couch. He patted the couch for me to sit down next to him.

"I think I found something," he said.

Sitting down next to him, I looked at the TV. He had the movie 'This Christmas' sitting up there with Idris Elba on the screen.

"Oh my God, I love this movie. How did

you know? Yeah, Idris Elba is my TV husband," I squealed.

Naveed cringed. "I'm doing this to thank you. Trust me, I'm really not into this kind of thing, but I wanted to express my thanks for you putting up with me during this time," he said before tapping the play button on the remote control.

We sat there and watched the movie and laughed. The funniest scene was where the woman was hitting her husband with a belt while he was scrambling to get up off of the slippery bathroom floor.

"Oh my God, this is hilarious. Who knew?" Naveed, let out a hearty laugh when she slapped him with that belt and ran.

"That's my favorite scene," we laughed for about five minutes. "Do you have any popcorn?" I asked.

"I believe I do. Look in the pantry to the left," Naveed instructed.

Looking to the left in the pantry, I found the popcorn and threw it in the microwave. I looked around in the spice cabinet, where I found the white cheddar popcorn seasoning. Yes, I knew he had this. Everyone I knew who had microwave popcorn had to sprinkle the white cheddar cheese on top. Grabbing a bowl, I put the popcorn in and sprinkled the seasoning on top. Grabbing two sodas out of the fridge, I headed back into the living room. I sat down and placed the sodas on the table in front of us. Naveed tapped play. We watched the movie, ate popcorn and laughed some more.

"I can't believe I've never watched that before. That was hilarious," Naveed said after the movie went off.

"I tried to tell you. Christmas is a very fun time of the year. There are so many hilarious Christmas movies on TV right now. I'm sure we could find another one. I mean, we could just turn it into a Christmas movie marathon because you need to get caught up, sir," I joked.

"Okay, but they have to be that funny because I don't know about those old corny movies that my grandmother used to watch," he laughed.

"Alright, I have another one for you. It's called 'Friday After Next.' This one is pretty funny too, so get ready!" I warned.

Naveed searched and found the movie on Amazon Prime. As the movie started, we finished the popcorn, this time laughing at Rickey Smiley playing a super skinny Santa Claus, robbing people, and running in slow motion through people's houses.

"Oh, my goodness, these movies are hilarious. I can't believe I've been missing out all these years," Naveed confessed.

By the end of the evening, I had snuggled against his chest, and we dozed off. The weird tension between us had worn off. I stirred when I felt Naveed pulling the cover-up over us.

"Are you okay? Do you need any Tylenol or something to drink?" I asked.

"No, I'm fine. I just wanted to make sure you weren't cold."

"I'm okay, thank you." Soon, I was fast asleep on Naveed's chest. It had been so long since I felt the warmth of another human body next to mine. I didn't want this to ever end.

The next morning, I woke up to just myself on the couch. Getting up to see where Naveed was, I wanted to make sure he was okay. I looked down the hallway to see if he was in the bathroom, but the bathroom door was open, so instead, I headed towards the kitchen.

"Sir, what are you doing in here?" I asked, knowing good and well, I could tell he was attempting to cook.

"I'm making you breakfast, can't you tell?" I looked over on the counter, and there was a box of Captain Crunch and milk sitting there.

I laughed. "You made me cereal? I love cereal, but it doesn't love me. I'm a little lactose," I joked.

"Oh Lord, I can't give you no cereal. You can't be in here pooting while we watch more Christmas movies today," he laughed. I went over to where he was standing and lightly slapped him on his arm.

"I can eat cereal. I just won't drink the milk, okay. Are you able to sit at this kitchen table?" I asked.

"I can. I might need a little assistance," Naveed hobbled over to the table using only one crutch.

"Naveed, you have to use both crutches, or you're not going to heal. There's no way you should be hobbling on one crutch. That's dangerous," I told him.

"No, I've been using both crutches. I just happened to set one down when I was trying to get the cereal out of the cabinet," Naveed said.

Once Naveed was sitting at the table, I moved the cereal, milk, bowls, and spoons over so that we could eat.

"Hey, do you remember reading the cereal box when you were a kid?" I asked.

"Yes, I used to love that, and I used to love reading the Happy Meal box when my grandmother bought me McDonald's," we laughed. "Yeah, those were the good old days, weren't they?"

"Sometimes I wish I was a kid again. Being a grown-up can be hard and lonely at times," Naveed confessed.

After we finished breakfast, I cleaned up the kitchen, which only consisted of a few dirty bowls and silverware.

"And sir, it is about time for you to have a bath. So, let me help you up, and I will go back here and run you a hot bath. Where do you keep your grocery bags so I can wrap that foot? You'll have to leave it hanging out of the tub."

"They're right under the cabinet over there," Naveed pointed.

I headed back to the bathroom and ran a hot bath. I knew he needed it. I noticed he had some men's shower gel, so I poured a little in for bubbles. I grabbed a candle and lighter that was sitting nearby, which I lit. Then I picked out a big fluffy towel and placed it in the bathroom.

"How are we going to do this?" Naveed asked.

"Well, you're going to strip, and I'm going to help lower you into the tub," I instructed.

"Okay, but if you drop me, I'm yours for life," he laughed.

"For life, hun? Don't tempt me," I laughed. I could get used to having a Naveed around. Noticing he was quiet. I looked up at him, and he put his lips to mine as we kissed.

"I'm sorry," he said immediately. "I hope I didn't weird you out."

"No, not at all," I answered.

Naveed braced himself against the wall and pulled his clothes off. I tried not to look, but I couldn't help it. I had to purposely tuck in my lips to stop them from spreading in delight. Naveed grabbed one of the crutches and put his arm around my neck as we scooted over to the tub.

"Okay, you're going to have to use a lot of your upper body strength. Now, I know you carry all those mail totes and parcels at work, so I know you have good arm strength." I joked.

We were lucky. The broken leg was the leg that would be on the outside of the tub, so he lowered his crutch after he stepped into the water then lowered himself, leaving the one leg out because it could not get wet. Once he sat in the water, he groaned in delight.

CHAPTER 10
NAVEED

MY GOD, THE COMFORTING HOT WATER SOOTHED my skin. I felt as if I hadn't had water on me in days. Leaning back in the tub to relax, I hadn't expected Blake to stay in the bathroom with me. But she picked up a washcloth and the bar of soap and washed my back, neck, and my hair. What have I done to deserve finding this gem? This woman who treated me so well?

"How does that feel?" Blake asked, allowing the hot water and suds to flow down my back.

"I've never been treated so well in my life. I'm thinking about the terrible way I acted with you for decorating my house for Christmas," I admitted.

We were both quiet. The only noise was water splashing as she dipped the washcloth in the tub and then washed my shoulders, neck, and back over again. The steam in the bathroom was intense. I sat there in such a melancholy mood. I looked up at her, and when I did this time, she pressed her lips to mine, and we kissed. Her lips were so delicate. The next thing I knew, I lifted her right into the tub with me.

"What are you doing, Naveed? You're getting water everywhere?" She said.

"Don't worry about it. I put my mouth over hers, closing the distance between us. We kissed over and over again until she pulled her wet clothes off and sat back in the tub between my legs.

You're beautiful," I whispered in her ear.

"Thank you.”

Kissing her neck gently, I used both hands to caress her breast. I squeezed, encircled, and pinched her nipples until they stood at attention. She groaned as I lifted her onto my erect manhood, anchoring my hands around her waist to pull her against me, I moaned.

We moved in a slow rhythmic motion, water rocking with us.

"*Naveed, please,*" she whined.

CHAPTER 11
BLAKE

Never in a million years would I have imagined I would be here making love to my mailman. He pumped into me with such ferocity.

"Oh my God," I groaned in delight.

Turning around, I straddled him, knees underneath forcing him deeper into me. We kissed, this time me riding the wave with friction. Water splashed everywhere, but we didn't care. At this point, we both needed that feeling. He nibbled on my tender breast as I drove him in delight.

Naveed's lips parted in pleasure, "*shit,*" causing me to bounce harder until our faces contorted, turning into screams of pleasure, then heavy breaths and throbbing.

"Damn B, what are you doing to me?" he whispered.

After we finished, I pulled the plug on the drain letting the water out, then plugging it back in and pouring another tub full of hot water, rinsing off again with soap and clean water. I rinsed us. I stepped out of the tub, first drying myself off the best I could, then I went back to the linen closet and grabbed more towels to dry the floor. After I got everything out of the way, I was able to help Naveed out of the tub. The last thing I needed was him slipping again on this wet floor. He got out. I propped him up on a crutch, and he held onto the counter. I'd dried him off from head to toe giving soft kisses along the way. Helping him into the bedroom, I got out clean undergarments for him and another pair of sweatpants, and a t-shirt.

Reclined back in his lazy boy chair, I gave Naveed some ibuprofen and a bottle of water so he could nap. I lay on the couch and took a catnap myself. When I woke up, I turned on the afternoon news and noticed that they had lifted the level three storm warning, and most counties were back down to level one. Gathering my things to leave, I knew it was time for me to get back to my life.

Naveed was sleeping so peacefully I decided to write a note. I didn't want to interrupt him. He'd used a lot of strength lifting himself and me into that tub this morning so, I thought it would be best to let him rest. After that, I tiptoed out of the house and headed on my way.

I stopped by the boutique to check on things. Most of the stores were either still closed or just starting to dig their way out. I parked in the back and went inside. Brielle was tagging some merchandise.

"Look who decided to finally show up for work," she joked.

"Well, did you expect me to come to work in a level three snow emergency and risk getting a ticket?" I said, hand on hip.

"Girl, you know I'm joking. Anyway, you needed to be over there with that man, and I see you look really relaxed today," Brielle noted.

I smirked.

"I'm only here because dad was going to

come to use the snowblower on the front sidewalk and parking lot. He should be pulling up any moment," Brielle said.

"Oh, here he is now," I headed to the front door to wave at my dad, who was unloading his snowblower. He waved back.

"I'm headed to your house after I finish up here," he said.

"Thank you, daddy. I love you," I yelled out the door before shutting it.

"Well, I doubt we get much business today, seeing as how most people are just trying to dig their way out of the blizzard," I advised. "I say once we get this inventory tagged and Dad finishes, we can close back up. I need to get Kobe from Bailey's house and get home. I haven't been home in days," I noted.

"Sounds good to me. I have some things I'd like to do today anyway," Brielle replied.

"Like what? Girl, it's a whole ton of snow outside," we laughed.

"I have things to do like catch up on my shows, that kind of stuff," she joked.

By the time Dad finished up, my sister and I were closing the shop. I hung the closed sign in the window that also directed people to the website and headed out.

My sister Bailey informed me that she was at our parent's home with Kobe. So, I followed Brielle back to our family home. When I got inside, Kobe ran straight to me.

"Hey boy, how are you doing?" I gushed. I bent down, scooped him up, and went into the main family room where my mom and Bailey were watching TV.

"Hey, Mom, hey Bailey."

"How are you?" Mom asked. Bailey waved.

"Oh, I'm good."

"How's that mail carrier? Is he okay?" Bailey asked.

"Yeah, he's recovering well," I responded.

"I don't know why you thought it was your responsibility to go over there and tend to that strange man," my mother responded.

"Mom, he's not a total stranger. We've been out before," I confessed.

"Been out for what? I hope you're not telling me you're dating the mailman," my mother hesitated.

"Mom, he's a decent guy," I defended.

"You know I've taught all of you girls to

marry so that you won't have to be worried about being broke," my mom pointed out.

Quiet, I didn't want to press the issue, realizing my mother's stance was never going to change. She had instilled marriages of convenience in us our whole lives.

"Now, I already told my friend Marge that you were going to bring her son to Christmas dinner. End of story," my mother objected.

I rolled my eyes and looked at my sisters, who cautioned me to be quiet.

"Okay, Mom, I gotta go," I added dryly.

"Let me get Kobe's things," Bailey chimed in, getting up off the couch.

FINALLY, AT HOME AND SETTLED IN, I CLIMBED into my bed and snuggled under the cover. Honestly feeling somewhat depressed about the situation, wanting to be loved, yet, scared to disappoint my mother. I mean, people had one-night stands all the time. There was nothing written in stone that Naveed and I were a thing anyway. We were both vulnerable in that moment, I tried to convince myself.

My phone buzzing pulled me out of my thoughts. I read the message.

Naveed: Why did you leave?

Me: I had to check on the boutique and get my dog from my sister. I'll be by in the morning with breakfast.

Naveed: Okay.

Not wanting to respond, I watched TV until I fell asleep.

The next day I got up and prepared myself for another day. Stopping for carryout, I picked up breakfast for Naveed and myself.

I called Naveed when I was on my way so he could unlock the door. Stepping out of my SUV, I picked up the bag of food and tapped on the door before entering.

"Naveed, it's me, Blake," I called out when entering the door.

"Come on," he said. "I missed you."

"Hey, sorry I left abruptly yesterday. You looked so peaceful I didn't want to interrupt you. I hope you're hungry?"

"It's okay. I am hungry now that you mention it."

We ate and enjoyed conversation over breakfast. He didn't know it, but me bringing meals was a way to continue spending time with this man. I wish we lived in a world where people paid more attention to each other's personalities instead of their status.

"You know Blake, I can't tell you the last time I had so much fun watching movies as I did the other night. It would be much appreciated if we could do something like that again," he said.

"I would love that. Let me just see what my schedule is looking like, and maybe we can have another movie night soon," I responded before checking my watch. "Well, I guess I better get out of here and head to the boutique. It's been closed for several days, and if I want to pay my bills this month, I should probably open up," I laughed.

"Feel free to call me later if you find a little time. You know I'm lonely out here by myself," Naveed added.

His comment had me raising my eyebrows.

"You look so beautiful," he added. I

jumped in his lap, showering him with kisses around his mouth and along his jaw.

"I really wish I could stay," I managed to say in-between kisses, "but, unfortunately, I have to go, adult, today."

"I know. I get it," he answered. I felt his erection lifting under me.

Gathering my things, I asked, "Do you need anything before I leave?" I asked.

"Don't ask if you can't fulfill," he laughed. "No, I'm good. I'm just feeling a little down. I'm not used to being stuck like this, but I'm going to rest and heal so that I can get back to my life as well."

"I know, I understand. I'll be glad when you get better too because then we can do other things like go on dates or go to the movies if that's okay with you?" I shrugged.

"Hell yeah," Naveed laughed.

I opened the front door turning the lock from the inside so when I closed it, the door would be locked.

CHAPTER 12
NAVEED

A COUPLE MORE WEEKS HAD PASSED OF ME BEING an invalid when I had finally gotten into my soft boot. Now, able to walk, my boy Ty picked me up for dinner and drinks at a local restaurant.

"Yo, man, thank you so much for getting me out of the house. Being sick and shut-in was starting to wear on me," I huffed.

"No problem, G. I figured it'd be nice to get out and have some dinner, drinks, and you know, shoot the shit," Ty stressed.

Taking a bite from my dish. I shook my head. "This shit is good," I mumbled, mouth full.

"I told you, fam," Ty was throwing down, too.

That's when she caught my eye. Blake and some nerdy looking dude were following a waitress to their seat.

I'm not going to lie. My mood was instantly ruined, but I tried not to jump to conclusions as to what I was seeing. I mean, we never did define that we were exclusive or anything, but we were starting to spend a lot of time together. I did sort of just pop in on her life, so I never considered the fact that she had other situations before me or not. It's not something we talked about. And truthfully, she could be on any type of date. It could be a business date or anything. Still, that feeling in the pit of my stomach begged to differ.

"You know, man, I'm getting to a point where I'm ready to settle down. You know there ain't nothing in these bars, same old gold-digging chicks. Every week trying to pull game you know what I mean," Ty sighed

"I feel you. I was kind of seeing someone myself, but you know I'm starting to think that was short-lived."

"Well, man, if it's anything like what I

have with my shorty, I say you stick with it cuz there ain't nothing out in these streets. That life gets old the older you get, feel me?" Ty stopped talking long enough to bite into his chicken.

Shaking my head up and down, I contemplated what Ty said. Still, I couldn't stop looking at Blake. I almost lost it when dude reached over to stroke her hand. That let me know what type of date it was. She moved her hand, but she was smiling. I couldn't gauge her emotions.

Ty spoke about his new love for another twenty minutes or so before I let him know I was ready to head out.

"Yo G, like I said before. Thank you, for getting me out. It was nice to get some fresh air, but I think I've been resting so much that I'm a little tired already. You know I'm still taking it easy," I explained.

"Yeah, I feel you. Let me get you back to the crib so you can get some rest," Ty added.

The ride back home was quiet. I felt bad because my boy was trying to get me in a better mood. But seeing Blake out there with that other man just messed me up. There was no way I could even pretend to be jovial at the moment.

Before stepping out of Ty's ride, I slapped hands with my boy thanking him again. By this time, I was so upset that when I got inside my place, I ripped down the Christmas decorations that Blake had put up for me. Not knowing what possessed me to do so but I wanted to hurt her for hurting me. I didn't know any other way to make that happen. It seemed Christmas was the only thing she ever expressed that made her happy. So, I pulled down the lights, the mini tree that she put up, and all the little trimmings, lugging it all outside and hurling them into the green dumpster by my house.

Livid, I moved inside and poured myself a stiff scotch on ice, and sat down to sulk. Thing is, I already knew from the way I was brought up that nobody sticks around. My parents didn't. My grandmother didn't, so why would I expect Blake to when I was literally nothing to her but the mailman.

Being around Blake felt good. It must have been the vulnerability of the moment when I made love to her to think there was something between us. My presumptions of how she felt could be blamed on the way she cared for me while I was down. Yet, how could I have been so wrong? Now, I know why I always dealt with the skanks from the bar because I didn't have a hard time sending them home the next day.

Blake was literally the first woman that I've wanted to spend time with. She was the first woman that I didn't want out of my face the next day. I genuinely looked forward to her bringing me meals. I blew out air. It was good while it lasted.

Now, I was anxious to get back to work and get back to my life. As a matter of fact, I was going to go back to work tomorrow. I don't care if they had to put me in a truck to drive mounted route. There was no way I could sit in this house another day alone.

CHAPTER 13
BLAKE

I WAS ANXIOUS TO WRAP UP THIS DATE WITH Marge's son Chris. He bored me to no end. Yeah, he was decent looking and had a bomb job, but he just didn't do it for me the way Naveed did. I could tell the first time Naveed smiled at me that I wanted to know more about him.

I flagged the waitress down. "Hey hun, I'd like a carry-out box. I'd also like to place a to-go meal, Ribeye steak, loaded baked potato, and broccoli," I confirmed.

"Let me put your order in, and I'll be right back with your container. Your meal shouldn't be too long. We're not very busy in the back," the waitress pointed out before walking away. She stopped at another table before heading to the back.

"You added a to-go box? You're very hungry, aren't you?" Chris rubbed his mouth with his napkin.

"Oh, don't worry, I'm paying for that. I'm going to take myself some lunch for tomorrow," I rolled my eyes while taking a sip of my sweet tea.

This date was so damn awkward and boring, the waitress couldn't get back fast enough with my to-go box and meal.

"So, I did six years over at Georgia Tech, well you know grad school, and an internship all of that combined," Chris boasted.

It sounded like blah blah blah to me. Like he was laying out a resume. He sounded stiff and rehearsed.

I'm glad I took my sister's advice and did a test run on this date with Chris because there's no way I could survive Christmas day with him. I wanted to feel comfortable on Christmas at home with my family without entertaining some bozo. I'm telling you that was the most genius advice my sister's ever given me.

Chris was still giving me his personal resume while I scrolled Facebook on my cell phone. He was such a dweeb. I guess I shouldn't say that he was a nice guy. He just wasn't my guy.

"Okay, hun, here is your meal to-go and your credit card. You two have a wonderful evening alright," the waitress gave her best 'please tip me' voice.

Chris stood up and headed around the table to pull out my chair and help me into my coat. That's one thing I could say was that he was a gentleman.

"Thank you so much, Chris, for this lovely dinner. I had a nice time," I told him.

"Did my mom mention something about us getting together on Christmas Day?" He asked.

"Oh no, that must have been a mistake. I already have plans for Christmas Day. But hey, you know, maybe I'll give you a call sometime if that's okay with you," I lied.

"That would be nice. I would like that," Chris buttoned his coat while I gathered my things, and we headed to the front door together.

We both handed the valet attendant the tickets to retrieve our cars.

"Oh, my goodness, it's gotten so cold out here. Now that the snow has stopped falling, the air is just frigid," I commented.

"Make sure you get buttoned-up. We don't need you getting sick out here in this cold night air," Chris almost sounded like a normal guy at that moment. Even though he was making small talk, it was much better than before when he was laying out his personal resume for me.

"Here's the attendant with my car. Okay, thank you again. It was nice meeting you," I hurried off to my vehicle because it was cold outside. Giving the valet attendant a tip, I jumped inside my ride. I appreciated the fact that the valet services warmed your car up before bringing it back.

Wanting to run this dinner by Naveed's house, I turned in the opposite direction I would have had I'd gone home.

I called my sister on the hands-free device in my vehicle.

"Hey girl, I just got off of that date with Chris. It was horrible," I laughed.

"Oh my God. Was he at least cute?" Brielle laughed.

"I mean, he was decent looking, but he

wasn't my cup of tea. The fact that he kept trying to give himself accolades. He spent the evening basically reciting his personal resume of how many years he spent here and what he did there and all of his charity work and blah blah blah."

"Oh, my God," my sister laughed. "Yeah, well, you know what you get when you date one of mama's friend's sons. I don't know why you didn't just tell her you had a date and then on Christmas just act like something happened and he couldn't make it. I mean, why put yourself through all this torture going on these horrible blind dates?"

"I don't know. Your guess is as good as mine," I blew out air.

We were both quiet. "Well, sis, I'm pulling up over Naveed's. I'm going to get off here now. Love you," I said, pulling into Naveed's driveway next to his vehicle.

"Girl, you going over there after you done got another man's cologne on you?" My sister joked.

I smacked my lips playfully. "Bye, sis. I'll see you at work tomorrow." I didn't have time to entertain her foolishness right now.

Naveed's house was dark. He hadn't

turned on the Christmas lights. But there was a light on inside. Stepping out of the vehicle, I grabbed the carryout bag and headed towards the front door. I rang the bell and stood there for a beat.

"Yeah," was all he said when he opened the door.

"Naveed, hey, how are you?" I asked, almost feeling as if I was at the wrong house. I turned around to look at the surroundings just to ensure I was in the right place. For some reason, he seemed cold and uncaring.

"Boy, it's cold out here. I brought you some carryout. I thought you might need something to eat," I said, trying to switch up the weird conversation.

"Are you really going to bring me leftovers from the date you just left?" Naveed stated coldly.

"Whaa, how did you know I was on a date?" I asked, wondering if he had been following me.

Naveed turned around, leaving the door open, so I followed him in. "What happened to all the Christmas decorations I put up for you?" I asked.

"I threw it all in the trash. Keep your dinner, too. I don't need your charity anymore. I'm fine. Now that I see, you tried to appease me to keep me from suing you, but I told you I wasn't worried about your money. I'm going back to work tomorrow, and we can go back to things the way they used to be between us. Non-existent!" Naveed headed back to the door and opened it.

Amazed to witness how cold he could be, I stepped out on the porch. I saw all the Christmas decorations piled up in the trash can. I don't know why because I'm not a crier, but for some reason, the tears busted out as I ran to my vehicle. This was one time I knew he wouldn't run after me because he had that boot on his foot. And I was happy he couldn't because I never wanted to see Naveed Peace again. I jumped in my car, peeled out fast, and headed home.

Naveed never even gave me an opportunity to explain to him that it was a blind date, and it meant nothing to me. I get it. I hurt him, but he hurt me too! Maybe my mom was on to something with these pre-arranged situations because if this was what love felt like, I didn't want to be loved.

Opening the door, Kobe ran straight to

me. Even on a bad day, I always had Kobe to come home to, and he always made things better. Stuffing the bag of food into the refrigerator, I really did have lunch for tomorrow.

After feeding Kobe and letting him out in the back to relieve himself, I was ready to call it a night. I felt like I was moving out of memory and habit. Nothing felt real to me at that moment. I showered and climbed into bed.

Looking at my cell phone, I silently hoped there would be a message from Naveed telling me that he made a mistake. But there was none. I started to compose a text to explain myself to him, but I couldn't make it make sense, so I put my phone down. Turns out, he thought I was treating him as a charity case so he wouldn't sue me. I guess that made me a one-night stand. I rolled over on my side and cried myself to sleep.

CHAPTER 14
NAVEED

THE NEXT DAY I GOT UP AND DRESSED FOR WORK. They were going to find something for me to do today because I was going crazy sitting in this house.

"Peace, hey, it's good to see you. Are you cleared to be back?" My supervisor asked.

"Well, obviously, I can't carry a route, but you can put me on a mounted route, and I can drive a vehicle since it's my left foot that's in a boot. I just can't deliver parcels or anything, but I can take the bulk of the load off somebody's back," I convinced him.

"Okay yeah, I can put you on mounted and put Harris on your regular route," my boss continued looking over his schedule. I headed over to case Harris's route.

"Peace, have a seat. He'll get it situated and loaded in the vehicle for you, and you can take it from there," my boss said.

"That sounds good." Happy he didn't make me provide documentation that I'd been released for work. I sat down at a station and pulled my cell phone out.

There was some part of me that really wished Blake would reach out. But I knew she wouldn't be the typical style of woman that was usually in my circle. I can't say that I've ever felt this way about a woman before. It was like I was addicted to her. I wanted to see her. I missed her coming around. I missed her laugh and her touch. But I would never play second fiddle to anybody.

"Peace. Go ahead to the vehicle and get started." Harris threw me the keys. Heading out to the vehicle, I looked forward to being preoccupied with some work and not sitting on my couch twiddling my thumbs for the day. That wasn't my life. I never was one to be lazy. I moved to the vehicle and headed over to the new area where I would be working. It was also good that I wouldn't be delivering mail to Blake. I didn't want to run the risk of running into her again.

The day was long, and I was still agitated even though I was preoccupied with work. I couldn't seem to get her off of my mind for shit. I mean, we literally only spent a few weeks together, but those few weeks I would trade for a lifetime.

Several days had gone by without a word from Blake and also without me sending her any messages. I guess it was over between us. Blowing out a sigh, I didn't want to be alone again, so I put on a pair of jeans and a sweater and headed back out to the neighborhood bar. Guess I'll go hang out with the crew and watch the game.

"Peace, hey, it's good to see you," my friend Ty greeted. I still couldn't understand how he was going to get married because he literally spent all his time and money in this bar. But that was none of my business.

Sitting down, the bartender handed me a beer without me even asking. It was kind of cool here, and this was the closest thing I had to family at the time. Still, in my feelings, I didn't want to be alone.

"What's the score?" I asked, taking a long

gulp of beer. I looked up at the TV. He told me, but it didn't really register. I was just making small talk. Not wanting to let on that I wasn't myself.

"Yo man, what happened the night we went to dinner? You were cool one minute. Next thing I know, you've just bottomed out on me. Do you have somewhere to go for Christmas? Because you know you can come hang out with me and my girl. She is going to do a little turkey, dressing, mac and cheese, and some pies."

"Oh man, I greatly appreciate that. Nah, I'm just going to chill. You know, probably order a carry-out from somewhere. I'm good. You need to spend some time with your lady and stop sitting in this damn bar every night," we laughed.

"Now you're starting to sound like Tammy. Whose side are you on anyway," he laughed.

"Well, man, I met a shorty a few weeks ago, and we were hanging out real tight for a minute, and then all of a sudden, the night you and I went out for dinner and drinks, I saw her at the restaurant with another guy," I shrugged and blew out air.

"Oh man, I'm sorry to hear that. You know these women nowadays. They ain't like they used to be," Ty noted.

"Yeah, that's why you need to get out of this bar and spend some time with your lady before you lose her," I told him.

"I'm supposed to be giving you advice, and you're here giving me advice. But you're right. I'm going to listen to you this time. I'm going to do better. Make it one of my New Year's resolutions," he confessed. "But man, you know women are a dime a dozen."

"That may be true, but for some reason, I can't get this one particular lady off my mind," I said.

The game came back on, and we quit talking to watch the last few plays of the night.

After watching the game for several minutes without saying anything, Ty looked over at me. "Yo G, if you think she's worth all that, maybe you should give her a second chance. Did you ask her about the person you saw her with, or did you just jump to conclusions?" He asked.

I was quiet.

"She didn't deny it, but then again, I'm

not sure I gave her an opportunity to give an explanation. However, old dude tried to rub her hand. That's why I jumped to conclusions. I didn't watch her exclusively. It's possible it was business. I don't know?" I tried to reason.

"Might do you good to just find out," Ty added.

"It's been several weeks. I think maybe just too much time has passed. Probably best if I keep to myself," I said. Why couldn't she have let me know if it was a business dinner? My mood was heavy all over again; I was wondering if Ty was right.

Sipping my beer, I blurted out. "Man, she decorated my house for Christmas, and at first, I fussed at her for crossing my boundaries. Later accepting that it was a nice gesture, I went along with it. But when she pissed me off that night, I ripped everything down and threw it in the dumpster. She ran away crying when she saw what I did. I doubt she'll ever give me the time of day again. Christmas was really important to her."

"Damn, man, you took down the decorations?" Ty let out a soft laugh while shaking his head back and forth. "That's messed up. You pulled down the lady's Christmas decorations without even finding out what happened first?" He laughed again.

"First off, I've never been in a relationship before, so I don't know how to act. Second, I'm used to these women from the bar and their one-night stands. None of them have ever taken the time to do anything for me. This lady nursed me when I was down, cooked for me, and washed my back. I'm just realizing that I might have messed that up for good."

"Damn, she did all that? I don't even think Tammy did all that for me before," he laughed.

I shook my head.

"What's her number? I'll call her if you won't."

CHAPTER 15
BLAKE

THE MORE TIME PASSED THAT NAVEED AND I hadn't talked, the more I realized that I missed and wanted him to be a part of my life. Still, I didn't know how to get around the situation with my mother, but I was convinced love had nothing to do with a person's status.

After doing some cleaning around the house, a different mailman walked up the steps to my porch. I opened the door seeing that he had a few parcels for me.

"Hi, hey, do you know Naveed, the mailman that's normally on this route? Have you heard anything about his broken leg?" I asked.

"Yeah, they put him on a mounted route where he drives instead of walking a route," he said.

"Oh, that's good, so he's doing better than?" I asked.

"Yes, I guess so. Where should I put these packages?" The new mailman asked.

"I'm so sorry. Here, I'll take those," I grabbed the packages from him.

Closing the door, I headed into the kitchen to make a cup of tea. After much contemplation, I got up and headed to my living room to grab one of the packages. It was a beautiful cashmere hat and scarf set. I wrapped it carefully and wrote out a hand-written note. I jumped in my vehicle and headed over to Naveed's. I took the Christmas package and stuck it in his mailbox, and then I headed to work.

At work, I tried to busy myself taking photos of the merchandise, knowing I had already done that. Yet, I was so preoccupied with my thoughts that I didn't realize what was happening.

"Like what is with you? You keep taking pictures of the same stuff. You've been sulking for days now. What is going on?" Brielle inquired.

"Well, I haven't really said anything, but Naveed and I were getting to know each other pretty well, and he saw me out with Marge's son Chris. Things got really heated between us, and we haven't talked since," I dropped my hands to my sides in defeat.

"Oh, my goodness, I'm so sorry to hear that, Sissy. Just tell him what happened," my sister said.

"It's not that easy. He never even gave me an opportunity to even explain myself. I had decorated his house for Christmas while he was down, and I guess he was so mad at me that he pulled everything down and threw it in the garbage. I've never been treated so horribly in my life. But I get it. We were making a connection, and I threw it away, trying to please everybody."

"I keep trying to tell you—"

"I cut my sister off saying it for her. "You can't please everybody."

She ignored the fact that I cut her off and kept talking.

"At some point in time, you're going to have to fall in love with who loves you. And you and I both know Mom doesn't believe in love," my sister confessed.

"I know. But Brielle, at one time, I honestly didn't think Mom's way of thinking was too far off, especially since I hadn't found anybody that I cared about. I just assumed it came with the territory. But now that I've met a man that I really care about, I don't see myself doing anything different. I'd almost rather be alone than spend my time with a man just because of his status. Does that make sense?" I asked.

"Yes, it does, and girl, trust me, no matter what mom says, I'm going to find a man that I really want to be with for the rest of my life." My sister continued to pack up an online order that she was filling.

Another full day went by, and I hadn't heard anything from Naveed. This time I wrapped a beautiful set of Sterling Silver cufflinks, wrote out another handwritten note and drove over to Naveed's house again, and put the gift into the mailbox. I was going to kill him with kindness.

Christmas was almost here, and my stomach was in knots. No longer worried about having a date to please my mother. I just wanted Naveed back in my life. Still, I had yet to hear from him. I was hoping he'd at least hear me out about what happened that night. And if he didn't forgive me, then so be it. I would move on.

A couple more days had gone by, and still no word from Naveed. I guessed he just wasn't going to forgive me. But at this point, I didn't care anymore. We've all made mistakes, and I'm sure he's not a saint either. It honestly ruined my mood for the holidays.

Tomorrow would be my last-ditch attempt to make things right with Naveed, and if he didn't comply, I guess I would give up on the situation. Tomorrow was his day off, Sunday, and then Monday was Christmas.

Sunday, I got up and went through my daily routine with myself and Kobe. Finally getting up the nerve to do what I set out to accomplish today, I hopped into my SUV and headed over to his house. On pins and needles at the prospect of seeing him again, I pulled up and knocked on his door. To my surprise, he answered.

"Hey," I said.

"Hey," he said back, never inviting me inside.

"I just want to say I'm sorry. I've tried in so many ways to express that I was sorry. I wanted to tell you this face to face about what happened that night."

"I'm listening," he said.

Wrenching my hands back and forth, I explained. "My mother was insistent on me bringing a date to Christmas. She'd already promised a friend of hers that I would bring her son. I didn't want to, Naveed. It's always been my plan to invite you to Christmas. So, to appease everybody, I went on a blind date with this guy. I had a horrible time because I thought about nothing but you the whole evening.

I was worried about whether you had something to eat or not, which is why I ordered you a meal. I'm so sorry. I know it didn't look good, but in my defense, you and I have never said that we were exclusive."

Naveed had his game face on, never giving me any indication that he was going to forgive me. In fact, all he did was push his hands down into his pockets.

Listen, I know this is your day off. And really, I just wanted to apologize and ask you if you would come to Christmas dinner at my parents' house tomorrow." Naveed stood there dumbfounded. I handed him the invitation and headed back to my SUV. He never even said more than two words to me.

At this point, I decided to let it go. I spoke my peace, and I guessed he just wasn't the right man for me.

CHAPTER 16
NAVEED

Don't ask me why we both stayed in that bar until it closed, especially Ty because he had someone to go home to. We moved as if we didn't have a care in the world until the owner told us to go home. Giving each other one last shoulder bump for the evening, we headed our respective ways.

Being that it was Christmas when I got home, I pulled out all of the packages that had been sitting in my mailbox over the past week. All of them from Blake, I'd never even opened them. Some little part of me wanted to have gifts to open on Christmas like normal people did.

Remembering how immediately I'd been

regretful the day I'd thrown away all the Christmas decorations away after Blake left my house crying. I'd gone outside and gathered them all up. I couldn't bring myself to throw the decorations away, even though I did nothing more but stuffed them into my hall closet.

Suddenly the twinge of regret turned into excitement when I retrieved the decorations from the closet. First, just observing them like the foreign objects they were, I realized it was almost dawn, and it would do me good to get some sleep at some point.

Feeding the weird mood, I was in, I decorated my place. Taking a bit of time to try and recreate what Blake had done for me, I finally lit the lights on my little Christmas tree. Arranging the Christmas packages, I received from Blake and placing them underneath. I snapped a picture. I sent the photo to Blake, captioned The Grinch Who Stole Christmas, brought it back. Thank you, and Merry Christmas, Blake.

With Christmas movies playing on my TV in the background, I sat down next to the tree. First, I unwrapped the smallest gift. It was a dope ass set of cufflinks. Something

I've never owned, however; I did plan on using them one day. Picking up the hand-written note, my eyes poured over its contents.

Naveed, I thought it might be fitting to explain to you that my parents raised me on the premise of marriages of convenience. I never thought it was weird or out of place until I fell in love with you. It took me going on that pre-arranged date that night to realize my heart did something different when I thought about and spent time with you. It was something I'd never experienced in my life. Sadly, you want nothing to do with me now, and I understand how I hurt you, and I'm sorry.

I folded the paper up, unable to finish. I was getting too emotional.

"*I drank too much tonight,*" I thought there wasn't much in life that could bring me to tears.

Opening the next package, it was a fly cashmere hat and scarf set. "Wow," was all I could say as I brushed my hand across the fabric.

"*So, this is what cashmere feels like, huh?*" I picked the scarf up and ran it along the side of my face. It was so soft. Again, I picked up the handwritten letter that went with this package.

Naveed, this is from Kobe. He wanted to thank you for saving his life. Which made me chuckle out loud.

This was my first time having any type of Christmas since my grandmother passed. Had I not been a fool, I might not have been alone today. I knew she was probably asleep, and honestly, I was dead tired myself, so I moved to my room, climbed in bed, and passed out.

CHAPTER 17
BLAKE

"I'm divorcing Christmas," were the words I said to my sister Brielle who was the first to call and wish me a Merry Christmas.

"Girl, you know Christmas is your Boo," Brielle joked.

"Not anymore," I sighed. I don't think I'm coming today."

"No, you have to! You know I can't take Mom and Bailey without you," she lied.

"I'll be there, but I can't guarantee I'll be there long," I confessed before ending the call.

For the first time in my whole life, I wasn't excited it was Christmas. Lying in bed with no will to get up, this must be what depression mimicked in others.

Kobe came trotting around the corner with a Christmas Package in his mouth.

"Awe, Merry Christmas, Kobe," I said almost in a whisper. Hell, even Kobe was ready to open gifts. However, I'm assuming he just smelled the doggie treats and knew it was something for him.

"You're so smart," I said, helping him unwrap his package.

Kobe was the one whose love for me never faltered. I was grateful to have my little pup.

Our family always unwrapped gifts together and knowing I was supposed to help with dinner. I mustered the will to get out of bed.

An hour later, I pulled up to the house I'd grown up in. Everything looked the same. Gathering gifts and treats, it took me several trips back and forth to my SUV to get everything moved inside.

"Merry Christmas," my family sang out when I entered my parent's home with all of my baked goodies and packages.

I forced out a "Merry Christmas."

"Come on in here and get some eggnog," my dad said, grabbing most of the stuff that I was carrying.

"Girl, I got a flask in my purse if you need something to spruce up the eggnog," my sister Bailey whispered, winking her eye.

"You can best believe I'm going to take you up on that," I smiled.

Sitting down around the tree, we passed out gifts to each other. Normally, this was my favorite part of the day. Trying my best to smile and not let on that I was feeling some kind of way, I moved through the holiday on autopilot.

Never in a million years would I have thought that I would be unhappy on Christmas yet, here I was feeling like I had a hole in my heart. Honestly, I couldn't wait for this day to be over.

It was almost time for dinner, and both of my sister's dates had shown up on time. I almost wanted to say I didn't feel well and go home. I couldn't think of anywhere else I'd rather be right now but under my covers. Both of my sisters looked happy with their dates.

Sitting by the tree after we cleaned up

all the extra wrappers, I picked up my phone to scroll social media and noticed a message from Naveed that I hadn't seen earlier.

Oh my God, he put the tree back up and added the gifts I gave him underneath with a caption The Grinch Who Stole Christmas brought it back.

That made me happy. Still, he never mentioned anything about accepting the invitation to dinner at my parents' house. The fact that he put the decorations back up warmed my soul, giving me a little extra pep in my step. Looking at how happy all of the couples were on Facebook and honestly, I'm glad I didn't have a blind date because I just really wasn't in the mood for it.

"Come on, Blake, you can help me get the food," my mother said. I picked myself up, ready to get this part of the day over with so I could go home.

Mother was checking the turkey when I entered the kitchen. "I think I'm going to give it about five more minutes," mother said, setting the timer on the stove. "I'm glad you're here because I want to have a word with you."

I pulled one of the high bar stools back from the island and sat down.

"You know I've been giving this some thought. I see how you've been moping around for weeks and I kind of heard through the grapevine that you and the guy you were seeing fell out," mom noted.

"Do we have to do this now, today, Mom?" I huffed.

"Now, hear me out. I know that I've instilled in you girls over the years more on status than love. But honestly, sometimes I think about it, and I wish I would have married the guy that I loved. Don't get me wrong. I love your father now that we've spent so many years together. I can't help but love him. But I often wonder where I would be now had I followed my heart?"

"Mom, how come you've never told me this," I asked.

"I honestly swept it under the carpet. I've been thinking about things lately when I noticed how sad you were and when I asked your sister about it, she told me that you and your friend fell out because you were trying to please me." Mom picked up a towel and wiped her hands.

"Mom, I appreciate what you're saying to me; however, I think I've already missed the bus. Naveed was so mad when he saw me out on that date with Marge's son that he hasn't said more than two words to me in weeks. I've tried everything, but at this point, I'm just going to move on and concentrate on my business." I swallowed hard, trying to hold back tears. Mama gave me a big hug.

"Don't worry. It will work out if it's meant to be." Interrupted by the timer on the stove, mom headed back to retrieve the turkey. Following her que, we took the dishes out to the big table and sat everything down. Everyone washed their hands and found their respective seats around the table.

I was surprised to find a package in my spot when I sat down. I looked around, noticing no one else had a Christmas package in their place.

Curious, I asked, "What is this?" I picked up the box, trying to figure out where it came from. "Is this something that should have been under the tree?" I asked, looking at my family for a clue.

"I believe that has your name on it," my father confirmed.

"Open it," my sister Bailey stated.

Carefully opening the package, there was a beautiful gold bangle inside with the inscription. 'You inspire me' inside.

Then the words "Postmaster" filled my ears.

"Whaa," I gushed, swinging my head around. I knew that voice anywhere.

"Naveed, what did you say?" I asked.

"I said, Postmaster. Remember you gave me homework? Well, I began applying for the position after our conversation that day, and I received confirmation from an email I read this morning. I am the Postmaster of the Columbus District."

Jumping out of my seat, I ran into Naveed's arms. I would have jumped into his arms, but I thought about his broken leg and decided against it.

"Congratulations," I whispered in his ear before we kissed.

"Ahem," my father cleared his throat. We all laughed. Grabbing Naveed's hand, I pulled him closer to the dinner table, where I was able to introduce him to my family.

"Have a seat, son. You're just in time for dinner," my father said.

The End.
Thank you for reading, and if you enjoyed this story, please consider leaving a review. It helps others find my work. Thank you.
Amber Ghe

Also by Amber Ghe

Reading Order

Dear Readers,

All of my series can be read independently of one another. However, most of them are connected, and if you read the series in the order, I wrote them, you'll discover more depth to the stories and characters. Some of your favorite characters make appearances in later series, so if you'd like to glean the greatest depth from my writing, here's my suggested reading order.

The Mergers & Acquisitions Series:

Mergers & Acquisitions (Book 1)

Game Faces On (Book 2)

Dreams Under Construction (Book 3)

The Dream Series: Can be read as standalone-spinoff characters from Mergers & Acquisitions (Book 1)

To Steal a Dream (Standalone)

Christmas Chance (Standalone)

Wait for Tonight (Standalone)

Mixfits Series: Conspiracy Series

Mixfits (Book 1)

Mixfits (Book 2)

The Sins of OG (Standalone)

Bliss Way Short Stories: Common theme; single parents who live on Bliss Way – not connected.

Bliss Way

Candid for You

Love Makes Scents (free)

The Billionaire Bae Series:

Family First (free)

Honor (Book 1)

Valor (Book 2)

Power (Book 3)

Spirit (Book 4)

Noble (Book 5) Coming Soon

Kisses from Paris spinoff from The Billionaire Bae)

The Doctor and his Curvy Controversy

About the Author

Amber Ghe is the author of the compelling 'Billionaire Bae' series, penning romance stories with a hint of sizzle and women's fiction. She writes about characters who examine their lives, hopes, fears, and motivations, characters that will linger with you long after the story is over. She dreams that the Billionaire Bae series will become an internet series or motion picture one day.

She's made it her mission to encourage healthy self-esteem, attitude, and woman empowerment. While practicing her daily mantra, Girl, 'Show up for Your Life!' she's decided to make that her movement. A jack of all trades, she loves to dabble in art, design, movies, and of course, reading.

Working a nine-to-five by day and author by night, she hopes to make it a full-time job one day. She currently resides in Ohio with her husband, where she is a full-time mom.

She's following her real passion by working on her subsequent novels.

www.booksbyamberghe.com